TUMBLEDOWN

For Joshua P.R.

———————

For my parents R.B.C.

Atheneum
Macmillan Publishing Company
866 Third Avenue, New York, NY 10022

Library of Congress Cataloging-in-Publication Data
Rogers, Paul.
Tumbledown.
Summary: In the village of Tumbledown where everything
is broken down, an announcement that the Prince
is coming to visit creates a flurry of fixing-up.

[1. Repairing – Fiction]   1. Corfield, Robin Bell, ill.
II. Title.
PZ7.R6257Tu   1988   [E]   87 – 11558

ISBN 0-689-31392-6

First American Edition
Printed in Italy
10 9 8 7 6 5 4 3 2 1

TUMBLEDOWN

Written by Paul Rogers
Illustrated by Robin Bell Corfield

Atheneum   1988   New York

This is the village of Tumbledown,
where nobody bothers when things go wrong
and nothing is ever fixed.

This is the church whose bell hasn't chimed,
  whose clock hasn't told the village the time
  for as long as folks can remember.

This is the gate to the village school
that fell off its hinges years ago
and the children all climb over.

This is the store where the door's so stiff
that it needs a push or even a kick
to get it to swing wide open.

This is the place where you climb down the bank
and cross the stream on a rickety plank.
You can still see where the bridge used to be
till one stormy night it was washed away
and just a few stones were left standing.

And this is the Tumbledown village hall
with its creaking door and shaky old steps
and its notice board with a note that warns:
"Watch out for the wobbly rail!"

So what a surprise when they heard the news:
the Prince was coming to Tumbledown!
Like wildfire the word went round –
"We must get everything fixed!"

The Prince was sure to visit the Church!
Up in the tower, old Granpa Williman
went to work to repair the clock.
But down below when it chimed the hour…

DONG!

What if the Prince were to visit the school?
Herbert Hicks went straight to work.
It didn't take long to fix the gate.
But when the children climbed over that day...

WHOOPS!

What if the Prince were to visit the store?
   Mrs. Dawley hammered and sawed
   till the door swung open quite smoothly.
   But when Mrs. Peabody pushed it next morning...

SMASH!

And what if he wanted to cross the stream?
It took Bill Botchit three whole days
to finish the bridge.
But when it was done and the plank was gone…

SPLASH!

Still, by the time they'd all helped out
everything worked that was meant to work,
and the village was just about ready.

The great day came. The Prince arrived.
He was shown the store, the church, the school.
But the thing that delighted him most of all
was the sight of the ramshackle village hall.

WATCH OUT
FOR THE
WOBBLY RAIL

He ran up the steps. He leaned on the rail.
   "Come up," called the Prince. "There's plenty of room!
It's the perfect place for a picture."

Slowly they crowded onto the steps.
"Smile please," the photographer said.
Oh what a day to remember!
But just at the moment the camera clicked...

One by one they got to their feet.
What a shock! What a mess! Was the Prince all right?
"Your Highness, we're ever so sorry!"

"Sorry! Why sorry?" the Prince replied.
"Finally, I know the reason why
you call this village Tumbledown!"